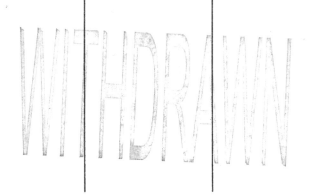

THE ADVENTURES OF
KING ROLLO

KING ROLLO AND THE NEW SHOES
KING ROLLO AND THE BIRTHDAY
KING ROLLO AND THE BREAD
KING ROLLO AND THE TREE

RED FOX

A Red Fox Book

Published by Random House Children's Books
20 Vauxhall Bridge Road, London SW1V 2SA
A division of Random House UK Ltd
London Melbourne Sydney Auckland
Johannesburg and agencies throughout the world

Copyright © David McKee 1979 & 1980

1 3 5 7 9 10 8 6 4 2

KING ROLLO AND THE NEW SHOES, KING ROLLO AND THE BREAD and KING ROLLO AND
THE BIRTHDAY first published by Andersen Press 1979
KING ROLLO AND THE TREE first published by Andersen Press 1980
Sparrow edition 1982. Reprinted 1983
Beaver edition 1986
Red Fox edition 1999

Printed in Hong Kong

RANDOM HOUSE UK Limited Reg. No. 954009

ISBN 0 09 929250 5

KING ROLLO
and the
new shoes

One day King Rollo visited the shoe shop.

He bought himself a new pair of shoes.

Of course, he already had shoes.

Kings have lots of shoes.

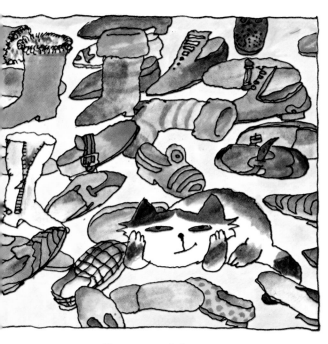

Lots and lots

and lots of shoes.

But King Rollo's new shoes were different.

His new shoes had laces.

King Rollo smiled and put on his new shoes.

"Do them up for me, please," he said to the magician.

"I can't always be around to do up your laces," said the magician.

"Make a magic spell to do them up," said King Rollo.

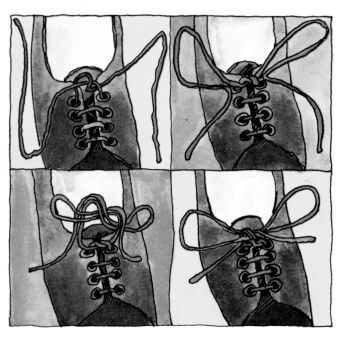

"A waste of magic. I'll show you how to do them up," said the magician.

"Left over right and under and pull. Make a little loop. Now make another. One loop goes over and under the other."

He repeated it with the other shoe.

"Just practise," said the magician, as King Rollo went into his room.

Soon strange noises came from the room. "Left over right and under and BLOW!"

And sometimes a sudden CRASH! like a thrown shoe.

"King Rollo has new shoes," the magician told the cook. "Lace-ups."

Later the noises were much quieter.

That afternoon Queen Gwen came to have tea with King Rollo.

The cook took her to King Rollo's room just as he came out.

"Oh," said Queen Gwen. "I do like your new shoes – they're lace-ups."

"Yes," smiled King Rollo, "and I did them up myself."

KING
ROLLO
and the
birthday

"Tomorrow is Queen Gwen's birthday," the cook said to King Rollo.

"Oh yes," said King Rollo. "I must send a birthday card."

He went to the shop to choose a card.

He bought the best card they had.

Then he went home to write inside it.

"That's not a very special card," said the cook.

"It was the best one they had," said King Rollo.

"Draw one yourself. It will be more special," said the cook.

"I can't draw," said King Rollo. "Try," said the cook.

King Rollo looked for his paper and paints.

He tried to think of something to draw.

He looked for a picture to copy.

"Draw Queen Gwen on a horse," said the magician.

King Rollo tried.

"It's awful," he said, and threw it away.

Then he tried again, and again.

"It's not as good as the bought one," he said.

"But it's much more special," said the magician. "Send it."

King Rollo posted the card.

Then he went home and tidied up.

The next day King Rollo was the first one at Queen Gwen's party.

Queen Gwen was pleased to see him.

"Thank you for your card," she said. "I loved it."

"It was very special," said Queen Gwen, "and it was different."

KING
ROLLO
and the
bread

King Rollo waved goodbye to the cook.

Then he and the magician went for walk in the country.

After a while, they met a farmer about to eat his lunch.

All the farmer had to eat was a loaf bread.

King Rollo wanted to show how clever his magician was.

"Would you like something different to eat?" asked King Rollo.

"No, thank you; the bread is fine," said the farmer.

"Roast chicken?" asked King Rollo. "Make the bread roast chicken, magician!"

With a flash, the magician turned the bread into roast chicken.

"Can I have the bread back, please? asked the farmer.

"Chocolate cake?" asked King Rollo. The magician changed the chicken to cake.

"Can I have the bread back, please? asked the farmer.

"Spaghetti?" asked King Rollo, and the cake was changed to spaghetti.

"Can I have the bread back, please?" asked the farmer.

"Ice-cream?" asked King Rollo, and the spaghetti was changed to ice-cream.

"Can I have the bread back, please?" asked the farmer.

"Well, what would you really like to eat?" asked King Rollo.

"Just the bread. It's delicious; my wife makes it," said the farmer.

"Give him his bread back," sighed King Rollo.

The magician turned the ice-cream back into the bread.

By now the food had made King Rollo feel hungry.

"Have some," said the farmer. "There's plenty here."

They sat side by side and ate the bread. It was delicious.

"Your magician is clever," said the farmer. "So is your wife," said King Rollo.

KING
ROLLO
and the
tree

King Rollo was in the garden.

"I'm going to climb that tree," he said.

"Don't climb the tree, you'll get your hands dirty," said the magician.

"I'm still going to climb that tree," said King Rollo.

"Don't climb the tree, you will tear your jacket," said Cook.

"I'm going to climb very high," said King Rollo.

"Don't climb the tree, you'll fall and hurt yourself," said Queen Gwen.

"I'm going to climb right to the top," said King Rollo.

Hamlet the cat said nothing.

King Rollo started to climb.

"Mmm," said the magician.

King Rollo climbed and climbed.

"Tut, tut," said Cook.

King Rollo climbed very high.

"Oh dear," said Queen Gwen.

King Rollo climbed right to the very top.

Then King Rollo slipped.

All the way down the tree he slipped and slid and slid and slipped.

Finally he landed on the ground with a BUMP!

"I said you would get your hands dirty," said the magician.

"I said you would tear your jacket," said Cook.

"I said you would fall and hurt yourself," said Queen Gwen.

"And I said I would climb to the top," said King Rollo.

"Yes," said Queen Gwen, "and you did."